THOSARATH PHOUMISAVANH

THREE KINGDOMS

A NOVEL

WINEPRESS WP PUBLISHING

WinePress Publishing (PO Box 428, Enumclaw, WA 98022) functions only as book publisher. As such, the ultimate design, content, editorial accuracy, and views expressed or implied in this work are those of the author.

Images used by permission of Art Resource; www.artres.com

Photo Credit : Erich Lessing / Art Resource, NY

Photo Credit : Alinari / Art Resource, NY

Photo Credit : Scala / Art Resource, NY

Photo Credit : Reunion des Musees Nationaux / Art Resource, NY

Image Copyright © The Metropolitan Museum of Art / Art Resource

© DeA Picture Library / Art Resource, NY

Photo Credit : Kimbell Art Museum, Fort Worth, Texas / Art Resource, NY

Photo Credit : Cameraphoto Arte, Venice / Art Resource, NY

Photo Credit : Bildarchiv Preussischer Kulturbesitz / Art Resource, NY

Photo Credit : The Philadelphia Museum of Art / Art Resource, NY

Photo Credit : Nicolo Orsi Battaglini / Art Resource, NY

© British Museum / Art Resource, NY

ISBN 13: 978-1-57921-996-3
ISBN 10: 1-57921-996-9
Library of Congress Catalog Card Number: 2008902188

Printed in Colombia.

The Land of Unity

Once upon a time, . . .

. . . peace and prosperity dwelled in a land called Unity. The fruits of the ground were many, and all were good for eating and for medicine. The two kingdoms that lived on the land shared the fruits of the trees, which gave life to all the peoples and magical beasts in the land of Unity.

3

About the Trees

The people and magical beasts of the land—who made up the two different kingdoms— lived in peace with one another and were thankful to the owner of the trees, who dwelled in the spiritual realm of the land of Unity. Thus, there were three kingdoms that lived and prospered in the land.

He Is All in All

The First Kingdom

The Kingdom of Power and Glory ruled in the beginning, before there were any people or magical beasts. It was the kingdom of creation, and all things flowed from it. The King, mighty and true, sat on the high throne. His son, the Prince, sat at the right throne and ruled the thousands of servants and workers under them to do the will of the King. The King gave his blessings to men and beasts throughout the land, and they honored the King and his Kingdom. On the left throne of the King were seven spirits of wisdom called the "Holy Council." The King, the Prince, and the Holy Council ruled the land and were of one mind, spirit, and will.

The Second Kingdom

The men who lived in the land were blessed with beautiful wives and many children. The husbands loved their wives, and the children were obedient to their parents. The parents led them in the way of peace, and every man lived as a king in his own household. The people of the land did not know of war or hate. All the people learned of peace from the first kingdom.

The Third Kingdom

The magical beasts lived on higher elevation closer to the mountains, where the trees gave life to all creatures. The magical beasts welcomed the people from the lower land when they came to gather food for their families from the trees. The people were always thrilled to see the magical beasts and fellowship with them, for they were very beautiful to behold.

The Fallen One

The blessings of the King went out to all the land and everything in it and also to the servants in the spiritual realm. The King's servants were blessed with awesome power and were able to do miracles in the land of Unity for the benefit of all creatures. Cain was the most blessed of all servants in the Kingdom of Power and Glory. But pride grew in his heart, and he used his powers for his own will rather than for his master, the King. All of the King's blessings made Cain self-righteous until Cain, the servant, began to believe that he should be king.

The Fallen Servants

Some of the other servants saw how Cain lifted himself up, and the same spirit filled their hearts to do the same. The other servants followed Cain. This act was very displeasing to the King, and he rebuked Cain in the presence of the whole kingdom. So Cain rebelled against the King, saying, "You will not rule over me!" Then there was a great war in the spiritual realm. The servants of the King fought and finally defeated Cain and his followers. And it happened that Cain and his followers were cast out of the Kingdom of Power and Glory.

Cain Lies to the Land

Now Cain and his followers fled to the land of Unity, where they once had served as workers for the King and the people. Cain now appeared to the people and magical beasts and said, "I am he who blessed you and provided for you, so give thanks to me, for I am king of all!" At the same time, the true servants of the King also appeared from the Kingdom of Power and Glory to rebuke Cain and let the people know what had truly happened. After this great confusion upon the creatures of the land, Cain fled away for a time. Great anger filled his heart, and destruction overtook his mind.

18

The King Warns the People

The King, knowing the heart of Cain, sent his servants to the people to warn them of problems to come. But because the people had experienced great prosperity in the past, many of them and the magical beasts did not believe the servants of the King. The servants warned of how and where the trouble would come, and those who believed fled from the area. Then it came to pass that Cain and his army cut down most of the trees in the land.

Trouble in the Land

When the trees were cut down, trouble came to the land of Unity. Cain then went out through the land, telling lies. He told the people that the magical beasts had cut the trees down, and he told the magical beasts that the King wished to see them destroyed. Sorrow and distress fell upon the creatures of the land, and they cried out to the King. So the King sent his servants to appear to the people. The servants said, "We will restore the trees, and we will put Cain in prison for your safety." The servants of the King began to grow new trees. But as the trees grew, Cain and his army cut down other trees.

Lack of Food

As the war went on and on between Cain and the King's servants, the people and the magical beasts became anxious and hungry. They began to gossip, and the lies that Cain had told them went out among the creatures of the land. Everyone had his or her own interpretation of what had been said. The trees that once freely fed the land were now items of great worth, and the creatures of the land sought to possess and control them. There was now enmity between the men and beasts. As the lack of food continued, some of the people began to hunt the beasts. And likewise, some of the beasts began to hunt the people for food.

24

A Promise

The King sent his servants to those who believed—the people and magical beasts who had fled to the place of safety. The trees that were there were untouched by Cain, and the fruits were plentiful. The servants said to the believers, "Listen to our words! Gather all the fruits from the trees and store them away for your journey to a better place. The King shall appoint a new leader from among you, and he will give your leader wisdom and power to guide and direct you to the place he has prepared for you. But be careful, because those who did not believe have become corrupt."

A New but Fallen Land

The unbelievers had now gone the way of Cain. Their hearts had become darkened, and the love of evil had grown among them. Because there was now enmity between the creatures, the people and beasts protected themselves by building walls and cities with the trees that had been cut down. The land of Unity was now divided. The spirit of pride entered into the people's thoughts, and they stopped giving thanks to the King who provided for them. The King saw that they were not the same creatures he once knew, so he withdrew his blessings. Cain saw that the people had forsaken the King, so he set himself up as their ruler.

The Chosen One

The Kingdom of Power and Glory mourned and grieved for those servants who had rebelled and been cast out. So the King said to the Prince, "I will fill my Kingdom once more. And I will bring the people of Unity who believed in me to my Kingdom, where there is much joy and prosperity." Then the Prince said to the King, "Please, Father, let me go down and be as one with them and teach them our laws, for they are weak and will become corrupt in time—not being able to keep your law of peace." So the King said, "Yes, you shall show them our ways. But first, let me send my Holy Council to them to prepare your way so that when you come to the people, both men and magical beasts will welcome you."

A Leader Is Chosen

Now it happened when the King's people and Cain's people lived alongside one another that the King's servants appeared to all men and magical beasts to proclaim a judgment on the land, because the people had gone in the way of Cain. However, the King's servants made a promise to forgive the people's rebellion if they would follow the King's chosen leader. Isaiah was chosen among all the people, because he hated the ways of Cain. The corruption of Cain's people had now spread to the King's people, and everybody saw the pleasure in seeking power and luxury for themselves at the cost of someone else. They would betray each other for it, and the stronger creatures would take advantage of the weaker ones.

The Heart of Isaiah

One day, Isaiah was distressed because he had just witnessed a crime. Someone had robbed his neighbor and taken his wagon of food that was to feed his village. The thief was looking to profit from it. Isaiah stood and watched, because he lacked courage and wisdom to help the victim and bring the robber to justice. As he was feeling troubled by this act, the Seven Spirits of Wisdom came to him in great beauty, and Isaiah was struck with fear and was paralyzed. But the peaceful power of the Holy Council overtook him, and he realized that he was called to servanthood for the King. Isaiah was then led out of the hustle and bustle of his village, up to the hills, and into a quiet place, where he was ministered to by the Seven Spirits of Wisdom, the Holy Council.

The King Revealed

Isaiah was told about the Laws of the King, which flowed from his very character. The seven spirits then revealed the character of the King. The first spirit proclaimed to Isaiah the perfection of the King and said that he is far superior to anything in the land. The second spirit proclaimed the sovereignty of the King and said that he has the power and the right to rule because all things flow from him. The third spirit proclaimed the King's justice and said that he will punish all wrongdoers. The fourth spirit proclaimed the King's mercy and said that he will forgive wrongdoers who come to him with a sorrowful heart. The fifth spirit proclaimed the faithfulness of the King and told Isaiah that he keeps his promises. The sixth spirit proclaimed the power of the King, stating that he sees all, knows all, and controls all. The seventh spirit proclaimed the eternal nature of the King, telling Isaiah that nothing can kill him, because he has no beginning or end and is even beyond time.

Journey to a New Land

The people now recognized that Isaiah was chosen by the King, and they wanted him to solve their problems. But Isaiah knew their selfish motives. So Isaiah said to them, "Trouble came to you because you were greedy. But I am here to bring you out of the land of Cain and into the land of Power and Glory." After this, some of the men and magical beasts followed Isaiah, while others stayed back in the land of Cain. The King set the people out on a two-year journey to test their faith and to grow in his laws. Isaiah then led the King's people out of the land of Cain—the land once called Unity.

A Government Is Formed

Isaiah's task was not a small one. So he handpicked some mighty men and magical beasts and set them up as commanders. Isaiah taught them the ways of the King, formed a government for the people, and gave them swords and armor to fight against any evil that would come from within or without. The ways of the King are love and peace, but evil must be fought with the same measure with which it attacks. Isaiah knew that if evil were not dealt with, it would spread like a wildfire and burn down the entire society. Now with law and order set for the King's people, each person was accountable to one another. Isaiah did all this because he saw the ways of Cain still in their hearts.

The City of Man

After the King's people left the land of Cain, the mighty men and beasts who remained followed Cain and took control of all the trees, rivers, and villages. They also took those who were weaker than them and turned them into slaves. The spirit of pride drove Cain and his servants to build large cities and monuments, which they dedicated to themselves. Cain favored the stronger slaves, and all the slaves competed with one another to get Cain's favor. In time, the weaker slaves became weary and died. So Cain said to his servants, "Let's go after those who left us and bring them back here to work for us. And let's kill Isaiah, their leader." So Cain's army pursued the King's people.

41

Guidance, Faith and Promise

As Isaiah led the King's people through the vast and foreign lands, he comforted them with promises the King had made about the new land they would enter. The people remembered the works that the King had done in the past and had hope in the future promises of the King. It pleased the King to see their faith and that they had put their hope in him. Isaiah said to the people, "I led you out of the land of Cain, but there is one who is coming whom I will anoint, and he will take you into the land of Power and Glory." Isaiah told both the men and magical beasts to trust the next leader, because he would be greater than he.

43

A New Leader

It came to pass one day that the Seven Spirits of Wisdom led Isaiah away from the people to a high hill. There, a baby was lying under the shade of a great tree with many fruits. The Holy Council said to Isaiah, "This is the Prince who comes from the right throne of the King. The King has given him to the people, and he has given the people to the Prince. This baby will grow in power and in glory and will lead the people to the King." Isaiah then went down to the people and proclaimed what had happened. So every man and magical beast went up to the hill to see the baby. There, Isaiah anointed the baby, and the people rejoiced and ate the fruits from the great tree.

The Battle

When Cain declared war on the people of the King, the Holy Council began to prepare Isaiah and the people for a fight. The powers of the Seven Spirits overshadowed the King's people, and they stood with great strength and courage. The army of Cain could be seen and heard from miles away as they approached. The Seven Spirits went out to Cain to talk him out of his madness, but Cain was not the same servant they had once known. Soon a great battle broke out, and many of Cain's servants fell by the sword. Cain threw a spear from afar at the baby—whom he knew the King had sent—but Isaiah jumped in between the baby and the spear, and fell to the ground and died. Cain and his servants fled from the battle, but Cain swore he would fight again.

Emmanuel Rises to Power

Sorrow and fear came over all the people as they buried their fallen leader. However, the people remembered Isaiah's words about the promised child. The elders of the people named the baby "Emmanuel," and all eyes were set on him as they went on day to day in faith. The people soon noticed great and awesome growth in Emmanuel. Unlike any man or beast, within months Emmanuel was already walking, talking, and teaching the people. Everyone said, "This child is supernatural." Emmanuel could do miracles such as heal the people and feed them with the same type of fruit they had eaten back in the land of Unity.

Opposition Arises

One day, some men and beasts among the King's people decided to challenge the leadership of Emmanuel because he was so young. Emmanuel understood that children should obey their parents, but he was no ordinary child—he was the son of the King, chosen to guide the King's people. So Emmanuel stood strong against their lies, because the truth was on his side. Emmanuel continued to guide and provide for the people, and those who argued with him were ashamed of their lies, because even they were provided for. Emmanuel's miracles only served to further prove that he was sent by the King.

The Church Is Established

Emmanuel said to the people, "Isaiah taught you how to fight against evil. But from today and to the days of my father's Kingdom, I will show you the ways of peace." So Emmanuel established a church and appointed leaders for it. He wrote down many laws and prophesies for the people on a big scroll. As the people read and learned the laws and prophecies, they became closer to Emmanuel and closer to their neighbors, both man and magical beast alike. They became closer to the King and his Kingdom than ever before. The people's hearts of stone became hearts of flesh when they learned about the King.

A Curse in the Land

When Cain and his surviving army returned to their land, they learned that the judgment of the King had come to the land of Cain and that every tree had died and every river had dried up. So Cain and his servants cursed the King and again went out to destroy the King's people. They hated the King and hated the Prince, Emmanuel, even more. Cain told his fallen servants and the men and magical beasts who followed him that the powers of the King were great, but that they should fight until death in order to demonstrate the pride and hatred in their hearts. So they marched on, looking for a fight once again.

Emmanuel Is Sacrificed

Emmanuel knew that Cain was on his way for another battle, so he warned the people. But now that the people were learning the ways of peace again, many did not want to fight. The army was small, and the people were afraid. So Emmanuel said to the people, "Do not fear. I will settle this matter myself." Alone, Emmanuel went out to face Cain in the battlefield. Cain then said to Emmanuel, "Your people will fall today." Emmanuel replied, "They will not fall. Neither will you nor your servants will fall by any sword." Emmanuel continued, saying, "You know that I have the power to destroy you all, but I will make you a deal. I give you my life in exchange for my people. You will let them go, and I will let you and your servants live." Cain agreed to this deal and took a sword and pushed it in through Emmanuel. Emmanuel fell down and died. All among the King's people who witnessed the killing were shocked and overcome with grief and sorrow. Cain's servants celebrated. Emmanuel had sacrificed his life to save his people, and the people had learned the mystery of love from his sacrifice.

John Three Sixteen

Judgment on Cain

As Cain and his servants went to conquer new lands, their spirit of celebration soon turned to fear when they noticed that the trees were dying and the rivers were drying up even outside of Unity. The curse of the King had spread beyond the land of Unity (which was now called land of Cain). This went on until Cain and all his fallen servants, the men and magical beasts, died from hunger and disappeared. The King had brought justice to Cain and his people.

Faith Restored

The people had now lost Isaiah and Emmanuel. The only thing left of them was the scroll that Emmanuel had written for the people. So the wisest men and beasts from the King's people read and studied the scroll. Then one day they read a prophecy from the scroll, which said:

The King will never forsake his people. He has given you his servants from his Kingdom and even his own son, Prince Emmanuel. The Prince has given you his life, but death cannot stop his guidance. The Prince will rise with the sun in the morning, and he will have power over the sun. So be strong and continue in faith and follow the sun, for then you will find my Kingdom.

A Sign of Hope

One morning when the sun rose, an image of Emmanuel appeared behind the sun. The image was brighter than the sun and had power over it. Emmanuel made the sun move in different directions, and the people followed the sun to his Kingdom. The people rejoiced when they realized that the King had not forsaken them. The King provided trees with fruits and rivers flowing with water along the way for their journey to the land of Power and Glory. The prophecy from the scroll had come to pass.

Arrival at the City

The day of glory had now come. The people stood at the pearly gates of the city of Power and Glory. Emmanuel, the image who was behind the sun, now descended into the golden city. The pearly gates opened, and the people saw that the city was very beautiful. There were roads made of gold and rivers as clear as glass that sparkled like diamonds. The trees of the land were as great as the one Prince Emmanuel had been born under, and the fruits were many. The fruits not only fed the people but also made them close to perfect, just like the King. Then a great voice was heard over the city that said, "Enter into my Kingdom, my people, and you shall find everlasting rest from your long and hard journey!"

The People Meet the King

Now all the wonderful servants of the King came down from the beautiful hills and greeted the people. The people were even more overwhelmed when they saw the King, the Prince and the Holy Council in their full beauty. And Isaiah stood by their side. The King then said to the people, "I am the creator and provider of all things. In the past I blessed you with many things, but you then failed to give me the glory. Instead, you listened to Cain's lies. But I still pursued you and called you to my blessings. I will welcome you with love, because I love my son, and my son loves you even on to his death. So come now, my people who believe in me, into my Kingdom. Live in peace and grow in grace." The people realized that this was a great gift from the King, and they gave him thanks and glory forever and ever. A great feast was set for all the people—men, magical beasts, and the servants of the king. The king was very pleased, and once again his Kingdom was filled just as he had planned.

The End.